WHERE THE CREEK RUNS COLD

Liddell Rayne

CONTENTS

Title Page
Prologue: The Last Goodbye 1
Part 1: Falling into Silence 4
Part 2: The Echo of the Past 26
Part 3: The Drowning Silence 33
Part 4: The Return to the Creek 42
Part 5: Goodbye, My Love 51
Part 6: Epilogue – Hello Again 59
About The Author 67

PROLOGUE: THE LAST GOODBYE

The sky was a dull shade of gray, a blanket of clouds stretching endlessly above the cemetery. Rain fell softly, not quite a drizzle but just enough to make the ground soggy, the drops sliding down the black stone of the headstones like tears. Lila stood still, her umbrella limp at her side, raindrops dampening her clothes and hair, but she barely felt it. She stared at the small gravestone in front of her, a name etched into the surface: *Emily Jane Clarke.*

Lila's hands trembled as she traced the letters, the cold stone beneath her fingers sending a shiver through her body. Emily. The name echoed in her mind like a faint whisper, a voice she hadn't heard in years but could still remember with aching clarity.

She closed her eyes. Her breath hitched, but the tears didn't come. They hadn't come in a long time. Instead, there was only the familiar numbness, the dull ache that had settled inside her chest the day Emily died and had never left. Lila opened her mouth, wanting to say something—anything—but the words stuck in her throat, choking her. What could she say that would make any difference now?

"Hello."

The word slipped out before she realized it, barely louder than a whisper. She wasn't sure why she'd said it—perhaps because that was all she ever wanted to hear from Emily. Just one more greeting, one more moment where she could turn around and see her sister standing there, alive, smiling, the way she always had before everything shattered.

But there was no response. There never was.

It had been ten years since Emily's death, and still, Lila hadn't found a way to say goodbye.

She knelt by the grave, her knees sinking into the wet earth, and rested her head against the cold stone. The silence pressed in around her, thick and suffocating. It was the silence that had followed her for a decade, trailing her through every room, every conversation, every night alone in her apartment. It wasn't just the absence of sound—it was the absence of Emily.

That day, Lila had let go of her sister's hand for a second too long, turned her back for just a moment, and that was all it had taken. She'd never forgive herself. How could she?

As Lila sat in the rain, she thought she heard it again—a faint voice, soft and distant, like a memory trying to surface through the fog.

"Hello."

She froze, her breath catching in her throat. It couldn't be real. It was just the rain, or the wind, or her own mind playing tricks on her again. But it sounded so much like her—like Emily. Lila closed her eyes tightly, squeezing out the thought before it could take hold. She stood up, wiping the mud from her knees. She didn't need this. She didn't need to chase ghosts. Emily was gone, and no matter how much she longed to hear her voice again, it wouldn't change the fact that Lila had failed her.

With one last look at the grave, Lila turned and walked away, the rain masking the sound of her footsteps, leaving only the faint whisper of a voice she refused to believe she'd heard.

PART 1: FALLING INTO SILENCE

The library was always quiet during Lila's shift. Quiet enough that she could hear her own heartbeat, feel the rise and fall of her breath as it echoed against the rows of untouched books. It was a forgotten place—a relic from a different time when people actually read physical books, and the scent of old paper was comforting rather than musty and forlorn.

The library, in many ways, was her sanctuary. The world outside continued to rush forward—loud, chaotic, and demanding—but in here, time seemed to stand still. The worn-out carpets, the dim lighting, and the endless stacks of neglected books created a cocoon of isolation where no one expected her to be anyone other than the quiet girl who signed in at the night shift and left without a word at dawn.

It was easier that way.

She sat at the circulation desk now, staring blankly at the rows of shelves ahead of her. Her fingers absently traced the edge of the wood, worn smooth by years of clerks just like her, their lives passing in the same stillness. The clock on the wall ticked softly—too softly to break the silence but enough to remind her of the time slipping away, second by second.

A stack of returned books lay untouched beside her. She should have logged them into the system hours ago, but she hadn't been able to focus tonight. Her thoughts kept drifting, circling back to that morning at the cemetery, to the name carved into the stone: *Emily Jane Clarke*. Her sister.

It had been ten years, and still, the name felt like a knife in her chest every time she saw it, every time she allowed herself to think about it. She had become an expert at avoiding those thoughts, keeping them locked away in the darkest corners of her mind, only letting them out in brief, controlled bursts when she thought she was strong enough to handle it.

Lately though, the memories had been slipping through the cracks. Ever since that moment at the grave, when she had whispered that single word —*hello*—and heard it echoed back, as if from the depths of her mind, she had been on edge. She had heard Emily's voice before, of course, in dreams and fleeting memories, but this time it had felt different. Closer. More real.

Lila shook her head, trying to clear the fog of her thoughts. She couldn't go down that road again. She had buried those feelings for a reason. It was the only way she had survived the last decade—by locking Emily away in the past, where she belonged.

But the past never stayed buried for long.

She sighed and reached for the top book in the stack, flipping it open to the inside cover. It was an old hardback, its pages yellowed and brittle, the corners dog-eared and frayed. The title—*The Forgotten Echoes of Time*—seemed almost ironic, considering how long it had likely been since anyone had picked it up. Lila logged it into the system, her fingers moving automatically over the keyboard. The familiar routine should have calmed her, but tonight it only heightened her sense of unease.

The fluorescent lights above flickered, casting odd shadows across the desk. Lila glanced up at them, frowning. They did that sometimes—another sign of how outdated the building was. Still, the flickering light, combined with the oppressive silence, made her skin prickle. She couldn't shake the feeling that something was watching her, lurking just beyond the reach of the light.

She rubbed her temples, trying to will away the tension building behind her eyes. It was just her imagination. She had been working too many night shifts, living too long in her own head, with nothing but the quiet and her memories to keep her company.

The phone rang, sharp and sudden in the stillness.

Lila jumped, her heart leaping into her throat. She stared at the phone for a moment, her mind scrambling to catch up. No one ever called the library at this hour. The handful of patrons who still visited during the day had long since gone home, and there were no employees here except for her.

Her hand hovered over the receiver, her pulse quickening. She didn't want to answer. Something deep inside her—a primal, instinctive part of her—warned her not to. It was just a phone call, nothing more, right?

She picked up the receiver, her voice barely a whisper as she spoke. "Main library."
There was a pause, a stretch of dead air that made the hairs on the back of her neck stand on end. For a moment, she thought she had lost the connection. Then, through the faint crackle of static, she heard it.

"Hello."

The word was soft, almost a whisper, but unmistakable. Lila's breath caught in her throat. Her grip on the phone tightened, her fingers trembling against the plastic. The voice... it was familiar. So familiar that it sent a chill racing down her spine.

"Who is this?" she asked, her voice shaking.

No answer. The static on the line grew louder, crackling and hissing in her ear. She waited, her heart pounding, but whoever was on the other end didn't speak again. Then, just as abruptly as it had started, the line went dead.

Lila stared at the phone in her hand, her pulse racing. She slowly set it back on the cradle, her mind spinning. It couldn't have been... She shook her head, trying to dismiss the thought before it could take root. It was just a prank, or maybe a wrong number. That's all it was.

The voice had been so clear. It had sounded so much like—No. She couldn't go there. Not again.

She stood abruptly, pushing her chair back from the desk. The air in the library felt too heavy, too still, pressing in on her from all sides. She needed to move, to shake off the feeling that had settled deep into her bones.

The rows of shelves loomed before her, dark and endless, stretching back into the farthest corners of the library where the light barely reached. The library was an old building, its architecture grand and imposing, but in moments like this, it felt more like a mausoleum—a place where things went to be forgotten.

Lila walked down one of the narrow aisles, her footsteps muffled by the thick carpet. The books around her were mostly untouched, their spines covered in dust, their titles long since faded. She could count on one hand the number of people who had checked out a book from this section in the last year. Most of them were older volumes—histories, encyclopedias, old collections of poetry. The kind of books no one read anymore.

She reached the far end of the aisle, where the shelves curved into a small, dimly lit alcove. It was her favorite spot in the library, tucked away from the rest of the world, hidden from view. No one ever came back here, and that was exactly why she liked it. It was her refuge, her hiding place.

She sat down on the small wooden chair that had been pushed against the wall, the seat creaking under her weight. The lamp overhead cast a faint, flickering light across the pages of the book in her lap, but Lila didn't open it. She couldn't focus on the words, not with the phone call still echoing in her mind.

"Hello."

Her heart clenched at the memory of that voice. It had sounded so much like Emily. She had been hearing it more and more lately—whispers in the back of her mind, fleeting snatches of sound that disappeared before she could be sure they were real. At first, she had dismissed it as stress, a side effect of working too many late nights and getting too little sleep. But now… Now, she wasn't so sure.

A creak from behind her made her jump. She whipped her head around, but the alcove was empty. She was alone, as she always was during these shifts. She took a deep breath, trying to steady her racing pulse. Her nerves were shot, that was all. She was jumpy, paranoid. There was no one here but her.

The feeling of being watched however lingered, a cold weight pressing down on her chest. She couldn't shake the sensation that something —*someone*—was just out of sight, lurking in the shadows beyond the reach of the light.

The flickering lamp cast long, shifting shadows across the shelves, making the books seem to move, their spines rippling like waves. The air felt thicker now, the silence no longer comforting but oppressive, suffocating.

Then, from somewhere in the distance, she heard the faintest whisper of a voice.

"Hello."

Lila froze, her breath catching in her throat. The voice was so soft, so quiet, that she might have imagined it. There it was, unmistakable, and this time, it wasn't coming from the phone. It was coming from the shadows beyond the shelves.

She stood, her legs shaky, her heart pounding in her chest. "Who's there?" she called, her voice trembling. The only answer was the sound of her own breathing, echoing in the stillness.

Lila backed away slowly, her eyes scanning the darkened rows of books. She had worked here for years—she knew every inch of this library, every nook and cranny. But now, the familiar space felt foreign, hostile. The shadows seemed to stretch and deepen, and the air grew colder, heavier.

Her back hit the edge of the desk, and she nearly jumped out of her skin. She was shaking now, her hands clammy, her throat tight. She had to get out of here. She needed to leave, to escape this suffocating silence.

Before she could move, the library door creaked open.

Lila's breath caught in her throat as a figure stepped through the doorway, silhouetted against the dim light from the street outside. He was tall, his coat dark and soaked with rain, his face shadowed beneath the brim of a wide-brimmed hat.

For a moment, they stood there, staring at each other in silence. Then the man stepped forward, his boots thudding softly against the floor. He moved slowly, deliberately, his eyes never leaving Lila's.

"Good evening," he said, his voice low and calm.

Lila's heart pounded in her chest. "Who are you?" she asked, her voice barely above a whisper.

The man smiled—a small, knowing smile. "My name is Samuel," he said. "And I think we need to talk."

Lila stood frozen, her mind racing. The man who had introduced himself as Samuel was tall, broad-shouldered, and carried an aura of quiet certainty that unnerved her. His voice was calm, but it cut through the thick silence of the library as if it had been meant to, like he knew he was supposed to be here at this exact moment. He didn't belong in the forgotten aisles of old books and dust—his presence was too deliberate, too real, for this place that had long felt like a sanctuary from the outside world.

Samuel stepped closer, his boots tapping softly on the worn floorboards. The shadows clung to him like he belonged to them, his dark coat melding with the dim light. He had removed his hat now, and Lila could see his features more clearly—sharp, but not unkind. His eyes, though, were the most unsettling part. They were dark, but not hollow—intense, and focused entirely on her, as though he could see straight through the protective layers she had built around herself over the years.

"What do you want?" Lila asked, her voice trembling, betraying the fear she had been trying to suppress.

Samuel's smile was subtle, a mere twitch of his lips. "I think you already know."

His words sent a chill down her spine, colder than the air in the drafty old library. She instinctively backed away, the desk pressing against her back. Her fingers gripped the edge, the wood digging into her palms as she tried to ground herself, to remind herself that this was real, that this stranger was just a man—nothing more, nothing otherworldly. Although, there was something in his gaze, in the way he moved and spoke, that unsettled her deeply.

"I don't know what you're talking about," Lila replied, her voice firmer this time, though her body betrayed her nerves with the tremble in her hands. "I don't know who you are, or why you're here, but you need to leave."

Samuel paused, his eyes narrowing slightly as if he were considering her words, weighing them. For a moment, Lila thought he might actually listen, that he might turn around and walk out the door the same way he had entered. But then he spoke again, his voice soft, patient, as though he were explaining something she had simply forgotten.

"I'm here because you've been hearing it, haven't you?" he said, his gaze never leaving hers. "The voice. You've been hearing it for a while now, but recently... it's become more persistent."

Lila's blood ran cold. The voice. The one that had whispered her name on the phone, the one she had heard at the cemetery, the one she had tried to convince herself was just a trick of her mind. Her heartbeat quickened, thudding loudly in her ears as the reality of his words sank in.

How could he know that? She hadn't told anyone—not a soul. She hadn't even fully admitted it to herself.

"I don't know what you're talking about," Lila said again, but this time her voice wavered, betraying her.

Samuel raised an eyebrow, his expression calm, almost pitying. "You do," he said gently. "You've been running from it for years, pretending that the silence is your friend. But it's not, Lila. It's not just silence you've been living with, is it? There's something else. Something you've buried."

Lila's stomach twisted painfully, and she felt a wave of nausea rise in her throat. She gripped the desk harder, her fingers turning white as she struggled to keep herself steady. How did this man know so much about her? How could he know about the voice, about the weight she had carried all these years?

"What do you want from me?" she whispered, her voice barely audible now, her throat tight with fear.

Samuel didn't answer right away. Instead, he glanced around the library, taking in the rows of books, the darkened corners, the flickering lights. His gaze settled back on her, and he sighed softly, as though he, too, were burdened by something unseen.

"It's not about what I want," he said quietly. "It's about what you need to do."

Lila's heart pounded harder. "What I need to do?"

Samuel nodded slowly. "You've been living in this place of silence, in this isolation, for too long. You've convinced yourself that if you don't listen, if you keep moving forward and ignore the past, it'll eventually fade away. But it hasn't, has it?"

Lila didn't respond. She couldn't. His words hit too close to home, cutting through the fragile defenses she had built around herself. Of course, the past hadn't faded—it had only grown stronger, more insistent. Emily's memory had lingered, no matter how hard Lila had tried to forget.

Samuel took a step closer, his voice soft but unrelenting. "The voice you've been hearing—it's not just in your mind. It's real. It's Emily."

Lila's breath caught in her throat. The world seemed to tilt beneath her, and for a moment, she thought she might collapse. She opened her mouth to deny it, to push back against the absurdity of what he was saying, but the words wouldn't come. Deep down, in the darkest part of her heart, she had always known. It was Emily. It had always been Emily.

"I… I can't…" Lila stammered, shaking her

head as if that would somehow undo the truth. "She's gone. She's dead."

"Yes," Samuel agreed, his tone even, as though he were discussing something as simple as the weather. "But that doesn't mean she's left you. She's been trying to reach you, but you've been too afraid to listen."

The tears came then, hot and fast, blurring her vision as she turned away from him. She couldn't bear the weight of his words, couldn't bear the weight of Emily's voice echoing in her mind, growing louder, more desperate. The voice had never been angry, never accusing, but it was filled with sorrow—a sorrow that matched her own.

"I don't know what to do," Lila whispered, her voice cracking under the strain of her emotions. She didn't care anymore that this stranger was here, witnessing her unraveling. The guilt she had carried for so long was too much, too heavy. "I've tried… I've tried so hard to forget, to move on, but I can't. I can't."

Samuel's expression softened, and he stepped closer, his voice gentle but insistent. "It's not about forgetting. It's about facing it. You've buried your grief, your guilt, for so long that it's taken root inside you. It's time to let it out. It's time to face her."

Lila shook her head violently, her tears falling freely now. "I can't," she sobbed. "I can't do that. I wasn't there for her, and now—now it's too late."

"It's never too late," Samuel said quietly. "Not for this."

The words hung between them, heavy and full of meaning that Lila wasn't sure she could fully grasp. She wanted to believe him, wanted to believe that there was still a way to make peace with the past, but the fear, the guilt, the crushing weight of responsibility—how could she ever let that go? How could she ever forgive herself?

Samuel watched her for a moment, his gaze steady, before he spoke again. "You need to go back."

Lila blinked, her tears momentarily forgotten. "Back?" she repeated, confused. "Back where?"

"To where it all began," Samuel replied, his voice low and calm. "You've avoided it for too long, Lila. You need to go back to the place where you lost her."

Lila's stomach twisted again, this time more violently. Her vision swam as the image of the creek flashed in her mind—the dark, cold water, the trees looming overhead, the sound of Emily's laugh just moments before it all went wrong. She had spent years avoiding that place, refusing to set foot anywhere near it. The thought of returning now, of confronting the very spot where her life had shattered—it was unthinkable.

"I can't," she whispered, shaking her head. "I can't go back there."

Samuel's expression remained calm, but there was a new intensity in his gaze, a quiet urgency. "You have to," he said softly. "Emily is waiting for you there. She needs you to come back."

The weight of his words pressed down on

her, suffocating, but at the same time, a flicker of something else stirred within her. Hope? No, it couldn't be that. Maybe it was the smallest spark of understanding, the faintest whisper of a possibility that she had never allowed herself to consider—that maybe, just maybe, facing that place could give her some kind of peace.

Lila swallowed hard, her hands trembling as she wiped at her tear-streaked face. Her chest ached with the force of her grief, but somewhere beneath that, a new resolve began to take shape. She didn't know if she could do it, didn't know if she had the strength to face what she had spent so long avoiding. But the alternative—living like this, haunted by the voice of her sister, trapped in a silence that was anything but peaceful—was no longer bearable.

"I don't know how," she whispered, her voice breaking. "I don't know if I can."

Samuel stepped back, his expression softening again. "You'll know when the time comes," he said quietly. "But it has to be soon. You can't run from it forever."

Lila closed her eyes, her mind spinning. She didn't know what to do, didn't know how to make sense of any of this. All she knew was that Samuel was right—she couldn't keep running. Not anymore.

When she opened her eyes again, Samuel was gone.

The library was empty once more, the silence oppressive in its finality. But this time, it wasn't the kind of silence that comforted her. It was the kind of silence that demanded to be broken.

Lila stood in the middle of the library, the weight of Samuel's words pressing down on her like an anchor pulling her to the depths. Her mind reeled, grasping for any thread of normalcy that could ground her. But normalcy had fled the moment she heard that voice on the phone. That single word—*hello*—echoed endlessly in her thoughts, louder now that Samuel had planted the seed of doubt, of truth.

She glanced around the empty library, its long aisles of forgotten books now seeming darker, the shadows deeper, and the silence heavier. There was something in the air now, something she hadn't noticed before—an oppressive stillness that felt charged, as if the very walls of the library were holding their breath. The rows of books, once a comfort, now loomed over her, like silent sentinels witnessing her unraveling.

Samuel had disappeared as suddenly as he had arrived, slipping away into the night like a shadow that had never been real. But his presence lingered, a phantom in her thoughts, his words repeating over and over like a mantra she couldn't ignore.

"You need to go back to where it all began."

Lila's breath hitched as the memory of the creek flashed before her eyes—the murky water, the overgrown reeds swaying along the bank, and the sound of Emily's laughter fading into the rustle of the leaves. She hadn't been back there since that day. She had promised herself she never would. To her, that place was the physical embodiment of everything she had lost, everything she had failed to protect. It was where her world had fallen apart, and she had locked it away, deep in her mind, behind walls so thick she had thought they would hold forever. But now, those walls were crumbling.

She sat back down at the circulation desk, her legs too shaky to keep standing. Her fingers clenched the edge of the desk as she stared blankly at the computer screen, its dull glow doing little to chase away the growing sense of dread pooling in her stomach. She couldn't focus, couldn't make sense of anything beyond the mounting pressure building inside her chest.

Emily is waiting for you.

Samuel's voice, calm and knowing, echoed in her mind. The more she tried to push it away, the stronger it became, as if it were being spoken directly into her ear. She shook her head, trying to clear the fog of emotions clouding her thoughts. It wasn't possible. Emily was gone. She had been gone for ten years. There was no *waiting*—there was only the past, and the crushing weight of guilt that had defined Lila's life ever since.

Her eyes burned as she blinked back tears, her heart pounding against her ribcage with a force that made it hard to breathe. The air around her felt too thick, too close. She had always loved the quiet, the stillness of the library—it had been her refuge for so long, a place where the world outside couldn't touch her. But now that stillness felt suffocating, oppressive, as though the very walls were closing in around her.

She needed to move, to do something—anything—to escape the spiraling thoughts that were dragging her deeper into the abyss of her memories. She stood up abruptly, the chair scraping loudly against the floor, the sound jarring in the overwhelming silence. Her breath was shallow, her pulse quickening as she paced behind the desk, her mind racing through a thousand thoughts but landing on none.

I can't go back, she told herself, her voice trembling in the quiet of the library. *I can't.*

Even as she said it, she knew it wasn't true. She had always known, deep down, that the past wouldn't stay buried forever. It had followed her, haunted her in ways she had never fully understood, and now it had caught up to her. The voice—*Emily's voice*—was proof of that. No matter how much she had tried to convince herself otherwise, Emily hadn't been silenced. Not really. She had been waiting.

A sudden gust of wind rattled the windows, startling Lila out of her thoughts. She looked toward the front entrance, half-expecting to see Samuel standing there again, watching her with those piercing, knowing eyes. But the door was shut, and the night outside was thick with rain, the droplets pounding against the glass in a steady rhythm. It felt almost like a warning, a reminder of the storm brewing both outside and inside her.

Her hands trembled as she reached for her phone, her fingers fumbling as she unlocked the screen. She had no one to call—not really. Her parents had drifted away years ago, consumed by their own grief, their own guilt. They had moved to another town, far from the memories, far from the weight of what had happened. They hadn't spoken about Emily in years, as though pretending she never existed would somehow make the pain go away.

And then there was Claire, her co-worker from the day shift. Claire had always tried to be there for Lila, in her own way, though Lila had never allowed her to get too close. She hadn't let anyone get close since Emily. But now, as she stared at her phone, her thumb hovering over Claire's contact, she hesitated. What could she possibly say? How could she explain any of this without sounding like she was losing her mind?

The phone screen dimmed as she dropped it back onto the desk, her chest tightening with the weight of her isolation. She had been alone for so long, trapped in her grief, and now that grief was threatening to consume her entirely.

The sound of footsteps broke the silence, startling Lila so abruptly that she nearly knocked her chair over. She whipped her head around, her eyes wide as she scanned the room, her heart hammering in her chest.

"Lila?"

The voice was familiar, and for a moment, a

surge of relief flooded her senses. Claire stood at the entrance to the library, her coat dripping with rain, her face drawn with concern. She must have come in through the side door, quietly enough that Lila hadn't noticed.

Lila let out a shaky breath, her body sagging with the release of tension she hadn't realized she was holding. "Claire," she breathed, her voice barely more than a whisper.

Claire frowned as she approached, her footsteps slow and cautious, as though she could sense the fragile state Lila was in. "Are you okay? I saw the light was still on, and I thought maybe you'd left it by accident."

Lila opened her mouth to respond, but the words wouldn't come. How could she explain what had just happened, how could she describe the weight pressing down on her chest, the voice that had whispered her name from beyond the grave?

Claire's frown deepened as she stepped closer, her eyes searching Lila's face. "You look like you've seen a ghost," she said softly, her voice full of concern.

A bitter laugh escaped Lila's throat, though there was no humor in it. She glanced down at the desk, her fingers still trembling as they clutched the edge. "Maybe I have," she whispered, more to herself than to Claire.

Claire blinked, her confusion deepening. "What do you mean?"

Lila shook her head, trying to steady her

breathing, trying to find the words to explain the inexplicable. But it all felt too surreal, too overwhelming. The phone call, the voice, Samuel's cryptic warnings—they all swirled together in her mind like a storm, threatening to pull her under.

"I've been hearing things," Lila said quietly, her voice barely audible. "Voices. Emily's voice."

Claire's face softened with sympathy, but her eyes remained cautious. She stepped closer, placing a hand on Lila's shoulder, a gentle but grounding touch. "You've been working too much," she said softly, her tone laced with concern. "You're exhausted. You've never really taken time off for yourself, not since—"

"Not since Emily," Lila finished, her voice cold and sharp, cutting through Claire's words. She didn't need to be reminded of that. She had been living it every day.

Claire nodded, her expression softening further. "I know you've never talked about it, Lila. Not with me, not with anyone. But you don't have to carry this alone."

The words should have comforted Lila, but they didn't. Nothing could. This wasn't something that could be fixed by talking or by taking a break from work. The guilt, the loss, the weight of Emily's memory—it was too ingrained, too much a part of her. And now, with Emily's voice reaching out to her from beyond the grave, it was clear that there was no escaping it.

"I don't think you understand," Lila whispered,

her voice trembling. "I've been hearing her. Not just in my head. I heard her on the phone. And..." She hesitated, the next words catching in her throat. "There was a man here. Samuel. He said I need to go back. That Emily's waiting for me."

Claire's brow furrowed, her eyes flickering with concern—and something else, something more cautious, like she was trying to gauge how far Lila had fallen into this dark spiral. "Lila, I think—"

"I'm not crazy," Lila snapped, her voice harsher than she intended. Her hands clenched into fists at her sides, her nails digging into her palms. "I know what I heard. I know what I saw."

Claire flinched slightly at the outburst, but she didn't back down. Instead, she placed both hands gently on Lila's shoulders, forcing her to look into her eyes. "I'm not saying you're crazy. I just think you're exhausted. You've been carrying so much for so long, and maybe it's starting to—"

"Starting to what?" Lila interrupted, her voice rising. "Make me lose my mind? Is that what you're trying to say?"

Claire's expression remained calm, but there was a flicker of something like frustration behind her eyes. "No, Lila. I'm trying to say that you've been running on empty for too long. And maybe now... your mind is trying to force you to deal with it."

Lila shook her head, her breath coming in short, ragged bursts. She couldn't listen to this. Claire didn't understand. No one did. This wasn't just exhaustion or burnout or unresolved grief. This was real. Emily's voice was real. Samuel was real. And the more she tried to deny it, the louder that voice became, tugging at her, pulling her back to the place she had spent ten years trying to avoid.

"I have to go," Lila muttered, brushing past Claire as she grabbed her coat and bag. She didn't know where she was going, didn't have a plan—she just knew she couldn't stay here, in this suffocating silence that was no longer her refuge.

"Lila, wait—" Claire called after her, but Lila was already out the door.

PART 2: THE ECHO OF THE PAST

The rain had slowed to a steady drizzle by the time Lila stepped outside, but the cold October air clung to her skin, biting at her cheeks and soaking through her coat. She hadn't grabbed an umbrella, hadn't thought to. Her mind was too crowded with thoughts, too overwhelmed by the voice she'd heard and the strange, unsettling presence of Samuel.

You need to go back.

Samuel's words echoed relentlessly in her head, just as Emily's voice had been echoing for weeks. No matter how hard she tried to push them away, they lingered, wrapping around her mind like vines, pulling her back to the place she had tried to forget. The creek. The woods. The day she had lost Emily. She couldn't go back. Not there. Not ever.

Lila walked aimlessly through the streets, her shoes splashing through puddles, her coat growing heavy with rain. The world around her seemed muted, the usual sounds of the city dampened by the weather and the late hour. Streetlights flickered in the mist, their orange glow casting long, distorted shadows on the wet pavement. She passed a few late-night walkers, but no one looked at her. No one noticed her. It was as though she existed in a bubble of her own—separate from the rest of the world, caught in the pull of something far darker, something only she could hear.

Her thoughts spiraled as she walked. She tried to make sense of what had happened—tried to rationalize it, to explain away the voice on the phone, the sudden appearance of Samuel. But there were no explanations. She had heard Emily's voice. She had seen Samuel. Besides somewhere, deep down, she knew that neither of those things were figments of her imagination.

Emily is waiting for you.

That sentence, above all, gnawed at her. Waiting for what? To accuse her? To condemn her for leaving her behind, for not saving her? For all the things Lila had been too scared to face?

The rain was falling harder now, drumming against the pavement with a rhythmic patter that matched the pounding in her chest. She didn't know where she was going—she had no destination, no plan—but her feet carried her farther from the library, farther from the safety of the familiar.

As she passed a narrow alleyway, a sudden gust of wind blew through the gap between buildings, whipping her hair across her face. Lila turned instinctively, shielding her eyes from the spray of rain. When she looked up, her heart stopped.

There, at the end of the alley, standing

perfectly still, was Samuel.

He was leaning casually against the brick wall, his coat pulled tight around him, his face shadowed by the brim of his hat. He wasn't wet, despite the rain. He wasn't cold, despite the wind. He stood there as if the world around him had no effect on him at all, like he was separate from it—just as he was separate from her.

Lila took a step back, her pulse quickening. "What are you doing here?" she demanded, her voice trembling. She hadn't expected to see him again, not so soon, not after the strange encounter in the library. She had hoped that leaving the building would somehow sever the connection, that the things he had said—the things he knew—wouldn't follow her out into the night.

Samuel didn't move. He didn't even blink. He just watched her, his expression unreadable, his eyes following her every movement.

"I told you," he said calmly, his voice carrying easily over the sound of the rain. "You need to face this. Running won't help."

Lila's hands clenched into fists at her sides, a surge of anger bubbling up inside her. Who was this man? What gave him the right to say these things, to know things about her that no one should know? She didn't understand him—didn't understand how he could know about Emily, about the voice, about the guilt that had been eating away at her for years.

"You don't know me," Lila said, her voice louder now, desperate. "You don't know what I've been through."

Samuel tilted his head slightly, his gaze never wavering. "I know more than you think."

Lila took a step closer to him, her frustration rising with every word. "What do you want from me? Why are you following me?"

Samuel pushed off the wall and took a step toward her, his movements slow and deliberate. "I'm not following you, Lila. I'm here to help."

"Help?" she scoffed, her voice cracking. "You're talking about things you don't understand. You're trying to tell me to go back to that place—" She broke off, her throat tightening, the memory of the creek surging to the forefront of her mind. "I can't go back there. I won't."

Samuel's gaze softened, but he didn't back down. "I know you're scared. I know you think it's too much to face. But you're wrong. You have to go back. Emily needs you to."

Lila's heart clenched painfully at the mention of her sister's name. The anger drained out of her, replaced by the familiar ache of grief, the guilt that had been with her for so long it had become part of her. She didn't want to hear this. She didn't want to believe it. But somewhere, deep in her heart, she knew Samuel was right.

"I can't," Lila whispered, her voice barely audible now. She could feel the tears welling up again, but she blinked them away, refusing to let them fall. "I wasn't there for her. I let her die."

Samuel's expression didn't change, but there

was something in his eyes now—something that looked like understanding, or maybe even compassion. He took another step forward, closing the distance between them, his voice low and gentle.

"You didn't let her die," he said softly. "It wasn't your fault."

Lila shook her head, her throat tightening with the weight of unshed tears. "I should have been there. I should have been watching her. I was supposed to protect her."

"You were a child," Samuel said, his voice steady. "You couldn't have known what would happen. You couldn't have stopped it."

Lila closed her eyes, her chest tightening painfully. She wanted to believe him, wanted to believe that what had happened to Emily wasn't her fault. But she couldn't. She had been there. She had been responsible. And she had failed.

The sound of the rain grew louder, pounding against the pavement, filling the silence between them. Lila wrapped her arms around herself, trying to block out the cold, the guilt, the relentless pull of the past. She couldn't do this. She couldn't go back. The thought of standing by that creek again, of reliving that day—it was unbearable.

Samuel's voice cut through the storm, calm and steady, anchoring her. "You think that by avoiding the past, you can outrun it. The truth is, it's been chasing you this whole time."

Lila opened her eyes, her breath shaky. She looked at Samuel, her vision blurred by tears, and for the first time since she had heard Emily's voice on the phone, she felt something stir inside her. It wasn't fear, or anger, or even guilt. It was something quieter, something deeper—a fragile thread of hope that maybe, just maybe, there was a way to find peace.

"I don't know how to go back," Lila whispered, her voice breaking.

Samuel took one final step forward, his hand reaching out to her. "You don't have to know how. You just have to be willing."

Lila stared at him, her heart pounding in her chest. His hand hovered in the space between them, an invitation, a lifeline. She wanted to take it, wanted to believe that there was still a way out of the darkness she had been living in for so long. The fear was still there, ever present gnawing at her, holding her back.

"I can't do it alone," she whispered, barely able to get the words out.

"You're not alone," Samuel said, his voice firm but kind. "I'll be with you."

For a long moment, Lila stood there, the rain pouring down around her, the world outside the alley muted and distant. She didn't know who Samuel really was, didn't understand why he had appeared in her life, but there was something about him that felt solid, real—like he understood her in a way no one else had.

Slowly, hesitantly, she reached out and took his hand.

The moment their fingers touched, Lila felt a strange sense of calm wash over her. The rain seemed to quiet, the cold fading just slightly, and for the first time in years, she felt a glimmer of hope. Maybe Samuel was right. Maybe she couldn't run from the past forever.

Maybe it was time to face it.

PART 3: THE DROWNING SILENCE

The next morning, Lila woke up with the weight of an impossible decision pressing down on her chest. She hadn't slept much; her dreams had been fragmented, haunted by shadowy images of the creek and the echo of Emily's voice calling out to her from beyond the water.

When the sunlight filtered through the thin curtains of her small apartment, Lila lay in bed, staring up at the ceiling, her mind churning. The previous night felt distant and surreal, yet Samuel's words had lodged deep inside her, his calm voice replaying in her mind.

"You need to go back to where it all began."

The thought of returning to the creek filled her with dread. It had been so many years since she had last stood there, but the memories were still sharp—so sharp they felt fresh, as if no time had passed at all. She could still picture the tangled branches overhead, the muddy banks where she and Emily had played, the dark, still water that had swallowed her sister whole. Even now, the image was enough to make Lila's throat tighten, her chest constricting with guilt and grief that had never truly gone away.

What choice did she have? The voice wouldn't stop. It had been growing louder and more insistent for weeks, and now Samuel had given form to her worst fears: Emily hadn't moved on. She was still waiting, still calling for Lila from wherever she had been trapped since the day she died.

Lila pushed herself out of bed, her body heavy with exhaustion and unease. The apartment was small, cluttered with books and papers, remnants of her life that felt strangely distant now, like pieces of someone else's existence. She moved through the familiar space on autopilot, her mind elsewhere, caught between the present and the past, between the world of the living and whatever place Emily's voice was coming from.

The drive to her childhood home took longer than it should have. The town had changed over the years—new stores, new houses, new people—but the road to her old neighborhood remained the same. It was as if that stretch of road existed outside of time, untouched by the progress of the world around it. The farther Lila drove, the tighter the knot in her stomach grew.

As the familiar landmarks passed by, each one stirred a different memory: the park where she and Emily had played, the old ice cream parlor where their father had taken them every summer, the faded sign for the elementary school they had attended together. These places, once filled with laughter and warmth, now felt hollow, abandoned in her memory like forgotten rooms in a house she no longer lived in.

When Lila finally reached the house, she parked a few blocks away, unable to bring herself to pull into the driveway. The house itself had been empty for years, ever since her parents had sold it and moved away. It looked the same as she remembered—small and unremarkable, with peeling white paint and overgrown bushes crowding the front porch. There was something about it that felt wrong now, as if the years of neglect had turned it into something darker, something hollowed out and haunted.

Lila hesitated for a long moment, her hands gripping the steering wheel. She didn't have to do this. She could turn around right now, drive back to the city, and leave the past where it belonged. Still, the memory of Samuel's voice lingered, pushing her forward.

"You're not alone. I'll be with you."

The words had offered comfort last night, but now, standing on the precipice of confronting everything she had tried to forget, Lila felt utterly alone. The weight of the years, the guilt that had grown into an ever-present companion, threatened to drown her before she even set foot inside the house.

Taking a deep breath, Lila opened the car door and stepped out. The air was cool, damp from the lingering effects of the previous night's rain, and the sky overhead was a dull, washed-out gray. She wrapped her coat tighter around herself and began walking toward the house, her footsteps slow and deliberate, each step feeling like an act of willpower.

The front yard was overgrown with weeds, the lawn forgotten long ago, and the pathway to the door was cracked and uneven, the concrete broken by the encroaching roots of the oak trees that lined the street. Lila's heart pounded in her chest as she walked up the steps to the front door, her fingers shaking as she reached for the handle.

The door creaked as it opened, the sound loud in the stillness of the house. Inside, everything was as she remembered it: the faded wallpaper peeling in places, the worn hardwood floors creaking underfoot, the empty rooms echoing with the ghostly memories of the life that had once filled them. The air smelled faintly of mildew, of time left to decay.

Lila stood in the entryway, her chest tightening as she looked around. This had once been her home, the place where she had spent her childhood with Emily, their laughter filling every corner. Now, it felt like a crypt—a place where the past lingered in the shadows, waiting to be unearthed.

She walked through the house slowly, her footsteps hesitant, as if she were afraid to disturb something that had long been at rest. The rooms were empty, stripped of furniture, but the memories were still there, etched into the walls and the floorboards. She could almost see it—the two of them, running through the living room, Emily's high-pitched giggle echoing as she chased her around the coffee table.

Lila's chest ached with the weight of it all. She hadn't allowed herself to remember these moments for years, had kept them locked away because it hurt too much to let them surface. Now, they came flooding back, each memory sharper and more painful than the last.

Finally, Lila reached the back door—the door that led to the woods behind the house, to the creek. Her breath caught in her throat as she stared at it, her hand hovering over the handle. This was it. The place she had spent ten years avoiding. The place where everything had changed.

For a long time, she just stood there, frozen in place, the memories swirling around her. She could hear the sound of the creek in her mind, the rush of water, the rustling of the trees. She could hear Emily's laughter, so clear and so close it was as if she were standing right next to her.

Beneath the laughter, there was something else. A voice. Emily's voice.

"Lila?"

Lila gasped, her hand jerking away from the door as if she had been burned. The voice wasn't in her head—it was real. It was here.

"Emily?" Lila whispered, her voice trembling,

the sound barely escaping her lips. She waited, straining to hear something, anything. Still the house remained silent. Her heartbeat thudded in her ears, drowning out everything but the rush of her own pulse.

She had to go. She couldn't stay in this house, couldn't let the memories pull her under. With a deep breath, Lila pushed open the door and stepped outside into the backyard.

The woods behind the house had grown wild in the years since her family had left. The trees were thicker now, their branches weaving together to form a dense canopy that blocked out most of the light. The ground was covered in wet leaves and tangled roots, and the smell of damp earth filled the air. It was darker here, more overgrown than Lila remembered, but the path to the creek was still there —faint but visible, winding through the trees like a scar etched into the land.

Lila's legs felt heavy as she followed the path, her breath coming in shallow gasps. Each step brought her closer to the place she had spent years trying to forget. The trees closed in around her, their bare branches swaying in the wind, creating the eerie illusion of movement out of the corner of her eye. The air was colder here, the shadows deeper, and with every step, the tension in her chest grew tighter.

When the creek finally came into view, Lila stopped, her heart pounding so hard it felt like it might break through her ribs. The water was dark and sluggish, reflecting the dull gray sky overhead. The banks were muddy, overgrown with reeds and brambles, and the sound of the water gurgling over rocks filled the stillness of the woods.

It was exactly as she remembered it—untouched by time, unchanged by the years. This was where it had happened. This was where she had lost Emily.

Lila's breath hitched as she stepped closer to the water, her eyes scanning the bank for any sign of what had happened here. There was nothing. Just the creek, flowing as it always had, indifferent to the tragedy that had unfolded on its shores.

She knelt by the water's edge, her hands shaking as she reached out to touch the surface. The water was cold, so cold it made her fingers go numb almost immediately, but she didn't pull away. She let the chill seep into her skin, into her bones, as if the cold could somehow bring her closer to Emily, to that moment when everything had changed.

"Emily," Lila whispered, her voice barely audible over the sound of the creek. "I'm sorry. I'm so sorry."

The words caught in her throat, choked by the weight of the guilt that had been festering inside her for so long. She had never been able to say it before—not to herself, not to anyone. But now, here, at the place where it had happened, the words came spilling out, unbidden and unstoppable.

"I should have been there," Lila sobbed, her voice breaking. "I should have saved you."

The wind rustled through the trees, but it didn't feel like an answer. It felt like an accusation. Like the earth itself was reminding her of her failure, her inability to protect the one person who had mattered most.

Then, through the rush of the creek, through the cold wind and the tangled branches, she heard it again.

"Why did you leave me?"

The voice was soft, childlike, but it cut through the air like a knife. Lila's breath caught in her throat as she scrambled to her feet, her eyes wide with fear and disbelief.

"Emily?" she whispered, her voice trembling. "Where are you?"

There was no response. The trees were silent again, the water flowing as it always had, but the voice—Emily's voice—lingered in the air, filling the space between the rustling leaves and the distant sound of the wind.

"You didn't say goodbye."

The words hung there, heavy with accusation and sorrow, and Lila's heart shattered. She had never said goodbye. She had never allowed herself to. She had buried her grief, her guilt, in the silence of the years, and now it had come back to claim her.

Tears blurred her vision as she fell to her knees, her body trembling with sobs. "I'm so sorry, Emily," she whispered, her voice hoarse and broken. "I'm so, so sorry."

The creek gurgled softly, the water flowing

steadily past her, but Lila stayed where she was, her hands pressed into the cold, wet earth. She had come here to find peace, to confront the past, but all she had found was the weight of her guilt, heavier now than it had ever been.

Emily's voice, calling out to her from the darkness.

PART 4: THE RETURN TO THE CREEK

The creek whispered its dark secrets as Lila sat frozen on the muddy bank, her knees pressing into the wet earth, her body trembling with the weight of all that had been left unsaid. The air was thick with moisture, each breath she took heavy and damp, as if even the atmosphere was conspiring to smother her under the burden of her own guilt.

"You didn't say goodbye."

Emily's voice still hung in the air like a ghost, the soft, childlike whisper cutting through the sound of the creek's steady flow. It was a voice that had haunted Lila's dreams for years, a voice that had once brought joy but now only served as a reminder of everything she had lost.

Lila's fingers curled into the cold, wet earth beside the water's edge, mud seeping between her fingers as she gripped the ground beneath her as if it could anchor her to something real, something tangible. Nothing felt real anymore. The past was bleeding into the present, the memories crashing over her like waves, threatening to pull her under.

"Emily," she whispered, her voice shaking. "Please… I'm here. What do you want me to do?"

The wind rustled through the trees again, carrying with it the faintest echo of that familiar laughter—a sound so soft, so distant, it made Lila's chest tighten with a longing so fierce she could hardly breathe. She had forgotten what Emily's laughter sounded like, the way it used to bubble up from her small chest like a song, pure and unburdened. How had she allowed herself to forget something so precious?

The answer was simple—because it hurt too much to remember.

Lila squeezed her eyes shut, willing the tears to stop, but they came anyway, sliding down her cheeks as the grief she had buried for so long finally broke free. She had spent years pretending that she was okay, that she had moved on, but here, at the creek, it was impossible to hide from the truth. Emily's death had shattered her, and the pieces had never fit back together the same way. She had been living a half-life ever since, going through the motions, never allowing herself to feel too deeply, because if she did—if she let herself feel—it would destroy her.

Now, though, she couldn't run from it anymore. She was here, at the place where it had all fallen apart, and there was no escaping the truth.

"Why did you leave me?"

The voice came again, clearer this time, closer. Lila's heart raced, her pulse thudding in her ears as she looked around wildly, her eyes searching the darkening woods for any sign of her sister's presence. Still, no one was there. Just the trees, the creek, and the creeping shadows of dusk. The air felt charged with something electric, something just out of reach, like the space between worlds was thinner here, more fragile.

"I didn't leave you!" Lila cried, her voice breaking. "I didn't mean to… I didn't mean for any of it to happen."

Her words echoed back at her, hollow in the stillness, but the air around her seemed to respond, the temperature dropping sharply as if the world itself was reacting to her grief. A chill ran through her, and she wrapped her arms around herself, her breath coming out in ragged gasps.

The creek, once a place of innocent play and carefree afternoons, had become a black mirror, reflecting back the worst parts of her memory. The water, dark and sluggish, seemed to hold the secrets of the past in its depths. It was here that she had turned her back, just for a moment—*just for a moment*—to chase after something trivial. A call, a distraction, and then… nothing. Silence. The sound of the water had swallowed Emily whole, leaving nothing but an empty space where her laughter had been.

Lila couldn't forget the way her heart had

stopped when she realized Emily was gone. She had raced to the water's edge, her feet slipping on the mud, her eyes scanning the creek for any sign of her sister. All she had seen was the stillness of the water, the way it flowed without care, indifferent to the tragedy that had unfolded in its depths.

The memories came flooding back now, sharper than they had been in years. She could hear the frantic pounding of her heart, the way her voice had cracked as she screamed Emily's name over and over, the rising panic as the minutes stretched on, each second a knife to her chest. Then, after what seemed like a lifetime, the sight of Emily's small, lifeless body pulled from the water by her father, his face pale with shock, his hands shaking as he tried to revive her.

It had been too late. Emily was already gone.

Lila let out a strangled sob, her hand flying to her mouth as the weight of that day crushed her once again. She hadn't saved her sister. She had let her die. She had failed her.

"I'm sorry," Lila whispered, her voice breaking under the weight of her tears. "I'm so sorry, Emily."

The wind picked up, swirling through the trees, and for a moment, Lila thought she saw something move in the shadows—something small, pale, and familiar. Her breath caught in her throat as she squinted, her heart pounding in her chest.

There, just beyond the creek, standing in the shadows of the trees, was a figure. Small, with long dark hair and a white dress that seemed to glow faintly in the fading light. It was Emily—exactly as she had been on that day. A child, frozen in time, forever eight years old.

Lila's breath hitched, her body going rigid as she stared at the figure, unable to move. It wasn't possible. Emily was dead. Gone. Yet, there she was, standing on the other side of the creek, watching her with wide, sorrowful eyes.

"Emily?" Lila whispered, her voice trembling.

The figure didn't move, didn't speak, but the air between them seemed to hum with an unnatural energy, a low, vibrating tension that set Lila's teeth on edge. The world around her felt too still, too quiet, as if the moment had stretched out into eternity, holding its breath, waiting for something to break.

Lila took a step forward, her heart racing. She wanted to reach out, to touch her sister, to pull her close and tell her everything she had been too afraid to say all these years. But as she moved closer, the figure seemed to fade, becoming less solid, less real, until she was nothing more than a shadow on the edge of Lila's vision.

"Don't go," Lila begged, her voice cracking. "Please, don't leave me again."

The figure flickered, like a candle struggling to stay lit, and then it was gone. The woods were silent again, the shadows deepening as dusk turned to night. The only sound was the steady gurgling of the creek and the soft rustling of the leaves in the wind.

Lila collapsed to her knees by the water's edge,

her body trembling with the force of her sobs. She had come here searching for peace, for closure, but instead she had found only more pain, more unanswered questions. Emily's voice still echoed in her mind, her words a constant reminder of everything Lila had failed to do.

"Why did you leave me?"

"I didn't," Lila whispered, her voice shaking. "I didn't leave you, Emily. I didn't mean to."

No matter how many times she said it, no matter how many times she tried to convince herself that it wasn't her fault, the guilt remained, heavy and suffocating. She had been the one who was supposed to watch Emily, to protect her, and she had failed. She had turned her back, and in that moment, everything had changed.

The darkness pressed in around her, the cold seeping into her bones as she knelt by the water. She didn't know how long she stayed there, her tears mixing with the damp earth, but eventually, the sound of footsteps broke through her grief.

Lila looked up, her breath catching in her throat. Samuel stood at the edge of the clearing, his face shadowed in the dim light, but his eyes were fixed on her, calm and steady. He didn't say anything at first, didn't move. He simply stood there, watching her with an expression that was neither judgmental nor pitying—just understanding.

"You came," he said softly, his voice low and quiet.

Lila wiped at her tear-streaked face, her hands

shaking as she tried to pull herself together. "I didn't know what else to do," she admitted, her voice hoarse. "I thought… I thought coming here would help. But it's just made everything worse."

Samuel stepped closer, his footsteps slow and deliberate, until he was standing beside her at the edge of the creek. He didn't speak for a long moment, his gaze drifting over the water, as if he, too, could see the weight of the past that lingered here.

"It's never easy," he said finally, his voice soft but firm. "Facing the things we've buried. The things we've run from. But you had to come back. You had to face it."

Lila let out a shaky breath, her hands clenching into fists in the mud. "I don't understand. Why is this happening? Why is Emily… why is she still here?"

Samuel knelt beside her, his eyes gentle as they met hers. "Because she never left. She's been waiting for you to come back. To say goodbye."

Lila's chest tightened, the words hitting her like a punch to the gut. "I don't know how to say goodbye," she whispered, her voice breaking. "I've been trying for years, but… I can't."

Samuel reached out, placing a hand on her shoulder, his touch light but grounding. "You don't have to let her go completely. Saying goodbye doesn't mean forgetting. It means accepting that she's gone, and that you did the best you could."

"I didn't do enough," Lila choked out, the tears falling again. "I let her die."

Samuel's grip on her shoulder tightened, just slightly. "You were a child, Lila. You couldn't have known. What happened wasn't your fault."

Lila shook her head, her heart aching. "But it feels like it is. It feels like I failed her."

"You didn't," Samuel said softly. "And it's time to stop carrying that weight. It's time to let her rest."

Lila's breath hitched, her body trembling with the force of her emotions. She wanted to believe him. She wanted to believe that it wasn't her fault, that she could find a way to let go of the guilt that had defined her life for so long. It was so hard, so impossibly hard.

"I don't know if I can," she whispered, her voice barely audible.

"You can," Samuel said, his voice firm but gentle. "And you don't have to do it alone."

For a long moment, Lila didn't move, didn't speak. She simply sat there, her mind racing, her heart heavy. The weight of the years pressed down on her, but slowly, something else began to stir within her. Something quiet, fragile—a faint glimmer of hope.

She had come here to find peace, and while it hadn't come in the way she had expected, it was possible. If she could face the past, if she could find a way to say goodbye to Emily, maybe she could finally start to heal.

With a deep, shaky breath, Lila nodded. She wasn't ready to let go yet—not fully—but she was ready to try.

Maybe, just maybe, that was enough.

PART 5: GOODBYE, MY LOVE

The wind whispered through the trees, carrying with it the scent of damp earth and decay, the unmistakable smell of autumn's slow crawl toward winter. Lila sat on the bank of the creek, her hands resting in the cold mud, her eyes staring blankly at the water as it rushed past, dark and steady, carrying away leaves and debris in its relentless flow. She could hear Samuel's breathing beside her, quiet and rhythmic, a steady reminder that she wasn't alone in this place of memories and ghosts. Still, she felt alone.

The weight of the past pressed down on her like a physical thing, wrapping around her chest and pulling her deeper into the grief she had been running from for so long. It was strange, how the place looked so unchanged after all these years, as if time had stood still, holding its breath, waiting for her to return. The trees were the same, the tangled branches overhead casting dark shadows across the ground. The creek flowed as it always had, indifferent to the tragedy that had unfolded here.

Only she had changed.

Her hands, now cold and covered in mud, were no longer the hands of a child. They were the hands of a woman who had spent ten years living with the weight of a loss she couldn't escape. She was no longer the girl who had played by this creek with her sister, carefree and unaware of how quickly life could turn. Now, she was someone else—someone shaped by grief, by guilt, by the burden of memories that had refused to fade.

The silence between her and Samuel stretched, thick and heavy, but it wasn't uncomfortable. His presence was steady, grounding. He didn't push her to speak, didn't demand explanations or force her to confront things before she was ready. He simply sat with her, his quiet understanding a balm to the raw wound that had opened in her chest since she had returned to this place.

"I don't know how to do this," Lila finally whispered, her voice so soft it was almost swallowed by the sound of the creek. Her throat ached from the effort of holding back her tears, her entire body tense with the weight of emotions she didn't know how to release.

Samuel didn't respond right away. When he did speak, his voice was as calm as the steady breeze rustling the leaves around them. "You don't have to know how. Sometimes, you just have to feel it. Let it come."

Lila closed her eyes, her breath catching in her throat. She had spent so many years trying not to feel, trying to keep everything locked away behind walls she had built up to protect herself. Those walls had crumbled the moment she heard Emily's voice again—the voice that had haunted her dreams, the voice she had heard on the phone, calling out to her from a place beyond the living.

"Emily," Lila whispered, her voice trembling. "I don't know if I can say goodbye."

The words hung in the air, heavy with the truth she had been avoiding for so long. It wasn't just that she hadn't said goodbye to Emily. It was that she hadn't been able to let her go. Emily had been frozen in time for ten years, preserved in Lila's memory as a little girl, forever laughing, forever young. That memory had also become a prison—one that Lila had built around herself, trapping her in the past, in the guilt of what she believed she had failed to do.

Samuel shifted beside her, his presence warm and steady. "Saying goodbye doesn't mean you're letting her go completely," he said quietly. "It doesn't mean forgetting her. It means letting go of the guilt that's kept you chained to this moment. It means finding peace, for both of you."

Lila's throat tightened. She wanted to believe him, wanted to believe that saying goodbye wouldn't erase Emily from her life, but the fear was still there—deep, gnawing, a fear that if she let go, she would lose her sister all over again.

"How do I let go of something like this?" she asked, her voice breaking. "I should have been there for her. I should have—"

"You were a child," Samuel interrupted gently, his voice firm but kind. "You did what you could. What happened wasn't your fault, Lila. You've been carrying the weight of this for so long, but it's time to stop blaming yourself."

Lila swallowed hard, her eyes still fixed on the dark water of the creek. She could feel the tears welling up again, blurring her vision, but she didn't wipe them away this time. She let them fall, let them trace the path down her cheeks, a small release of the grief that had been choking her for years.

"I don't know how to forgive myself," she whispered, her voice barely audible.

Samuel was silent for a long moment, and when he finally spoke, his voice was soft, almost reverent. "Forgiveness isn't something that comes all at once. It's a process. A choice you make, again and again, until one day it gets a little easier. But you have to start somewhere."

Lila's chest ached with the weight of his words. She knew he was right—knew that forgiveness, both for herself and for the past, wasn't something that would come easily. Nevertheless, if she didn't try, she would never move forward. She would stay trapped in this cycle of grief and guilt, forever haunted by the memory of Emily, forever hearing her voice calling out from the darkness.

She took a deep breath, her hands still buried in the mud, and let the silence settle around her. The creek flowed on, the water dark and smooth, as if it had no care for the human sorrow unfolding on its banks. It had always been that way—indifferent, uncaring. The creek had taken Emily, and the world had continued without pause.

"I miss her," Lila whispered, the words slipping out before she could stop them. "I miss her so much."

Samuel nodded slowly, his gaze softening. "I know."

Lila closed her eyes, the tears falling faster now. "I didn't think it would hurt this much after so long. But it never goes away, does it?"

"No," Samuel said quietly. "It doesn't. However, it does change. The pain becomes something you carry, something that shapes you, but it doesn't have to control you."

Lila's hands clenched into fists in the mud, her nails digging into the cold, wet earth. She wanted so badly to believe that—to believe that the pain of losing Emily didn't have to define her life. After ten years of living with that pain, she wasn't sure she knew how to be anything else.

"What if I don't know how to be without it?" she asked, her voice trembling.

Samuel didn't hesitate. "You'll learn. You'll learn to carry the love without the guilt, the memories without the pain. It will take time, but you'll get there."

Lila didn't respond. She couldn't. The ache in her chest was too deep, too raw, and the tears blurred her vision until all she could see was the water before her, dark and unyielding. She had come here to find closure, to say goodbye, but now that she was here, she didn't know if she could.

Then, through the fog of her grief, she heard it again—*Emily's voice*.

It was faint at first, barely more than a whisper on the wind, as Lila focused, the sound grew clearer. It wasn't the voice of a ghost, angry and accusatory. It wasn't the voice of a child who had been lost, crying out for help. It was the voice of the sister she remembered, the sister who had loved her unconditionally, who had followed her everywhere with wide eyes and endless admiration.

"Lila."

The sound of her name, spoken in that familiar, soft tone, made Lila's heart ache. She closed her eyes, letting the sound wash over her, and for a moment, she could almost feel Emily's presence beside her—small and warm, like she had been on all those afternoons they spent by the creek, laughing and playing without a care in the world.

"Emily," Lila whispered, her voice trembling. "I'm here."

The wind stirred, rustling the leaves overhead, and in that moment, Lila felt something shift inside her—a loosening of the knot that had been wound so tightly in her chest for so many years. The grief was still there, the pain of loss still sharp, but beneath it, there was something else. Something softer. Something like peace.

"You didn't leave me."

The words were so quiet, so faint, that Lila wasn't sure if she had imagined them. They were there, lingering in the air, carried by the wind and the gentle sound of the creek.

For the first time in years, the sound of Emily's voice didn't fill Lila with guilt or shame. Instead, it filled her with warmth—with the memory of love, of the bond they had shared that couldn't be broken, even by death.

Lila took a deep, shaky breath, her hands finally unclenching from the mud. She didn't have to hold on so tightly anymore. She didn't have to carry the burden of her sister's death like a punishment. Emily hadn't blamed her. Emily had loved her, and that love was still there, even now, echoing through the years, through the silence.

"I love you, Emily," Lila whispered, her voice thick with emotion. "I always have."

The wind whispered through the trees again, and for a moment, Lila could have sworn she heard the faint sound of laughter—Emily's laughter—bright and pure, like it had been all those years ago. It wasn't a haunting sound. It wasn't a cry for help. It was just... a memory. A memory of something beautiful, something that had once brought so much light into Lila's life.

She opened her eyes, the tears still falling, but this time, they weren't just tears of sorrow. They were tears of release—of letting go of the guilt, the shame, the weight of the past. The grief would always be there, although it didn't have to consume her anymore.

Beside her, Samuel stood, his gaze still fixed on the creek. He didn't say anything, but his presence was enough. Lila didn't need words. She didn't need explanations. She had found what she had come here for.

She had found peace.

For a long time, they stood there together in silence, watching the water flow, listening to the soft rustling of the trees, the distant echo of a voice that was no longer angry, no longer filled with sorrow.

Finally, Lila stood, her legs shaky but steady. She looked down at the creek, at the water that had once been a source of so much pain and took a deep breath.

"Goodbye, Emily," she whispered, her voice soft but steady. "Goodbye."

With that, she turned and walked away from the creek, her heart lighter than it had been in years.

PART 6: EPILOGUE – HELLO AGAIN

The sun was low in the sky, casting a soft, golden light over the cemetery as Lila stood by Emily's grave. The headstone was simple, worn around the edges by time and weather, the letters still clear but softened, like a memory that had been held for too long. *Emily Jane Clarke*—the name still had the power to bring a sharp ache to Lila's chest, but it wasn't the suffocating pain she had once felt. It was softer now, a bittersweet echo of what had been lost but never truly forgotten.

She knelt by the grave, her fingers brushing gently over the cool stone, her breath steady as she let the quiet settle around her. It had been two weeks since she had gone back to the creek—two weeks since she had said goodbye. In that time, something inside her had shifted. She still carried the grief, still felt the weight of her sister's absence, but the guilt that had haunted her for so long had begun to fade, replaced by a quiet sense of acceptance.

The world had kept turning, as it always did. The library still stood, silent and filled with the musty smell of old books, and Lila still went to work each night, but there was a lightness to her now, a sense that she was no longer walking through her life like a ghost. She had reconnected with her parents, reaching out to them after years of silence. The phone call had been brief, awkward at first, but as they spoke, Lila had felt something she hadn't felt in a long time—hope. Hope that she could rebuild the connections she had lost, that she could heal, even if the process was slow and painful.

She wasn't running anymore. She wasn't hiding. What is more here, by Emily's grave, she felt a quiet sense of peace.

"I came back, Emily," Lila whispered, her fingers tracing the letters on the headstone. "I said goodbye."

The wind stirred gently, rustling the leaves of the nearby trees, but the cemetery remained still, serene. There was no voice calling out to her now, no echo of guilt or accusation. The haunting presence she had felt for so long had lifted, like a weight being taken from her shoulders.

She placed a bouquet of white lilies at the base of the headstone—Emily's favorite flower. She remembered the way her sister had always picked them from the garden, her small hands clutching the delicate petals, her face lighting up with joy whenever she presented the flowers as a gift to their mother. It was one of Lila's favorite memories, one she had kept tucked away, afraid to look at too closely. Now, as she set the flowers down, she allowed herself to remember without fear, without the sharp sting of regret.

"I'll never forget you," Lila whispered, her voice soft but firm. "I'll always love you. But I'm going to try to live again."

As the words left her lips, she felt something—an almost imperceptible shift in the air, a lightness, as if the space around her had breathed with relief. It wasn't a supernatural presence, not the way Emily's voice had been before, but it was something—an acknowledgment, a release. Lila stood slowly, brushing the dirt from her knees, and looked up at the sky. The sun was setting now, casting everything in a warm, golden glow that softened the edges of the world.

She felt, for the first time in years, like she could breathe.

The cemetery was quiet as she turned to leave, the gravel crunching beneath her feet as she made her way toward the wrought-iron gate that marked the entrance. As she walked, her mind wandered—thinking of the future, of what lay ahead now that she was no longer bound by the chains of her guilt. She had no clear plan, no roadmap, but she didn't need one. For the first time in a decade, she felt ready to move forward, to let life take her where it would.

As she approached the gate, a figure standing in the shadow of the large oak tree by the entrance caught her eye. At first, she didn't recognize him—his dark coat blending in with the deepening shadows, his posture relaxed but watchful.

However, as she drew closer, the familiarity of his presence settled over her like a warm blanket.

Samuel.

Lila's breath caught for a moment, a mix of surprise and relief flooding her chest. She hadn't seen him since that day by the creek—since he had guided her through the most difficult moments of her life. She had wondered, in the days following, if she would ever see him again, or if he had simply been a part of that moment, someone who had appeared to help her through her grief and then disappeared into the ether.

Now, here he was—solid and real, standing by the gate as if he had been waiting for her all along.

Lila hesitated for a moment, then approached him, her footsteps light against the gravel path. "Samuel," she said softly, her voice carrying through the quiet of the cemetery. "I didn't think I'd see you again."

Samuel smiled—one of those small, knowing smiles that seemed to convey so much without words. "I told you I'd be with you," he said gently. "I wasn't going to leave you alone."

Lila's heart swelled with gratitude, and she nodded, though a part of her couldn't help but wonder—who *was* Samuel, really? He had appeared out of nowhere, seemingly knowing more about her life, her pain, than anyone else. He had guided her, comforted her, but he remained a mystery. And now, standing here in the fading light of the cemetery, the question tugged at her more than ever.

"Who are you?" Lila asked, her voice quiet but steady. "I mean, really. How did you know all of that about me? About Emily?"

Samuel's expression didn't change, but there was something in his eyes—something deep and ancient, as if he had lived a hundred lifetimes before this one. He looked at her for a long moment, his gaze gentle, before he finally spoke.

"I've been helping people like you for a long time," he said softly. "People who are lost. People who are stuck, like you were, unable to move forward. Sometimes it's grief. Sometimes it's guilt. But the story is always the same—they need someone to guide them back to themselves."

Lila's brow furrowed. "But why me? Why now? And how did you know about Emily?"

Samuel's smile deepened, though it was tinged with sadness. "I've known about Emily for a long time," he said. "You've been carrying her with you all these years, keeping her close, but also keeping her in a place where neither of you could find peace."

Lila's heart thudded in her chest, her mind racing. "Are you…?" She trailed off, unable to finish the question.

Samuel seemed to understand what she was asking. He shook his head slowly. "I'm not a ghost, if that's what you're wondering. I'm not Emily, either. But I've been sent to help people like you find what they've lost."

Lila's breath hitched, her mind struggling to grasp what he was saying. She had always felt that Samuel was different—there had always been something about him, something otherworldly, even though he looked like any other man. Standing here in the fading light, she realized that he was more than just a guide. He was something else entirely.

"Sent by who?" Lila asked, her voice barely above a whisper.

Samuel's eyes darkened slightly, but his smile remained. "That's not for you to know. Not yet anyway."

Lila stared at him, her heart pounding. She wanted to ask more, to press him for answers, but there was something about his presence—something that told her she wouldn't get any more than what he had already given. He was here to help her, to guide her, but beyond that, he was a mystery she wasn't meant to solve.

After a long moment, Lila sighed, her shoulders relaxing. "Thank you," she said softly. "For everything."

Samuel nodded, his expression warm. "You're welcome. You've come a long way, Lila. I'm proud of you."

Tears stung her eyes at the unexpected kindness in his words. She had spent so long believing she had failed, believing she was unworthy of forgiveness or peace. But here was Samuel, this mysterious figure who had somehow seen her pain and guided her through it, telling her that she was worthy—that she had done enough.

"Will I see you again?" she asked, her voice tinged with hope.

Samuel's smile softened, and for the first time, Lila thought she saw something like sadness in his eyes. "Perhaps," he said quietly. "But if not, know that you're not alone. You never were."

With that, he turned and walked away, his figure blending into the deepening shadows of the cemetery until he disappeared entirely, leaving Lila standing by the gate, her heart full but her mind swirling with unanswered questions.

She stood there for a long time, watching the spot where Samuel had vanished, the wind tugging at her hair, the fading sunlight casting long shadows across the ground. She didn't know what to make of him, didn't know if she ever would. For the first time in a long time, it didn't matter. Samuel had given her what she needed—closure, peace, and the strength to move forward.

Lila turned toward the grave one last time, the lilies swaying gently in the breeze. A sense of calm settled over her, the kind of calm that came from knowing that she had faced her past, that she had said goodbye, and that Emily was no longer waiting in the shadows, no longer calling out to her from the darkness.

For the first time in years, Lila felt free.

As she walked away from the cemetery, the world around her felt brighter, lighter. The weight that had once pressed down on her chest was gone, replaced by something new—hope. She didn't know what the future held, didn't know where her path would take her next, but she was ready to find out.

In the quiet of the evening, as she left the cemetery behind, she thought she heard it again—just for a moment—the sound of a soft, familiar voice.

"Hello, Lila."

A smile tugged at the corners of Lila's lips, and for the first time in a decade, she felt like she could smile without guilt, without the shadow of her past hanging over her.

"Hello," she whispered back, her voice filled with love.

Lila walked forward, toward the light, toward her new beginning.

ABOUT THE AUTHOR

Liddell Rayne

Liddell Rayne is a passionate writer with a love for storytelling. Whether crafting tales of adventure, horror, or fantasy, he finds joy in weaving words that captivate and inspire. Writing isn't just a hobby but a way to explore diffent worlds and share unique experiences with others.

When not writing, Liddell enjoys spending time outdoors, birding to connect with nature, or diving into the immersive world of video games. These intrests fuel their creativity, offering endless ispiration and fresh perspectives of their stories.

Made in United States
Troutdale, OR
05/13/2025